CW01583014

Sophie has been reading and writing books since she was eleven. She has been writing stories on and off for years but never turned them into a full book. Finally, after finishing her degree, she wrote her first full novel.

Elaine

All the best

S. al8[illegible]

For my mum, who gave me my first historical romance when I was eleven and started my obsession.

Sophie Culshaw

# His Little Flower

Austin Macauley Publishers™
London • Cambridge • New York • Sharjah

A CIP catalogue record for this title is available from the British Library.

ISBN 9781788787802 (Paperback)
ISBN 9781788787819 (Hardback)
ISBN 9781788787826 (E-Book)

www.austinmacauley.com

First Published (2019)
Austin Macauley Publishers Ltd
25 Canada Square
Canary Wharf
London
E14 5LQ

# Chapter One

### 19 February 1813, London

Mary was bored. She'd been bored for the last hour and a half but until now her mother had kept her promise to not send every unappealing, dreary and downright old gentleman her way. Until now that is, as her mother was currently talking to the Earl of Hallamshire and, very unsubtlety Mary thought, pointing at her. Mary hoped her mother had just stopped to chat with the man and not, as Mary feared, decided to play matchmaker. The man was old enough to be her father for heaven's sake! And it was said, mainly by gossiping servants, and then, just as much so by the older ladies when they thought no one was listening, although never directly to the earl and never directly to Mary, that the earl was a mean drunk. That particular piece of ever-present gossip must have escaped her mother's bat-like ears as, while her mother desperately wanted to see Mary married, Mary knew that Oliva Heron, the Countess of Winchcombeshire, would never want her children to marry someone mean.

Mary supposed that at three and twenty, and therefore very much on the shelf, she should be glad there were still gentlemen who wanted to dance with her, even if they were old and had wandering hands. Such was the case with the Earl of Hallamshire the last three times they'd danced since the start of the season.

"Mary!" Turning at the sound of her name, Mary saw her mother and the Earl of Hallamshire walking towards her.

"Miss Heron," murmured the earl as he bowed and kissed Mary's hand.

Mary bobbed a polite curtsey, "My lord, how lovely it is to see you again."

"Mary, the Earl of Hallamshire was wondering if you would accompany him in the next dance."

Mary looked at her mother and tried to show her displeasure without being too obvious.

"Yes, Miss Heron. I'd be delighted if you would be so inclined."

Seeing no way out of the situation, and knowing that her mother's sparkling green eyes, which were the image of her own, were firmly fixed on her, she dared not decline. So she placed her hand on the earl's extended arm and smiled politely at the ageing man. "Of course, my lord," she said, "that would be lovely."

Later that evening, Mary feigned needing to retire to her room and was now wandering around an abandoned corridor all the while trying desperately to forget how the earl's hands had wandered during their dance. His hands had been placed on her back more often than not during their dance; it was amazing really that he'd even managed that, as the Quadrille was not usually a dance that allowed for intimate touching – unwanted or otherwise.

"Oof!" So lost in her thoughts, Mary slammed into what felt like a wall. Closing her eyes, Mary braced herself for the impending impact of her bottom on the hard ground. Strong arms snaked around Mary's middle and her face was then pressed into a crisp cravat.

"You should look where you're going more often, little flower," drawled an amused voice above her.

At five foot, seven inches, Mary was uncommonly tall, and to have a man be above her height was unusual.

Looking up, Mary found herself drowning in very familiar, very blue, eyes. It took only a second for her to remember why the nickname, voice and eyes were so familiar.

"You!" Struggling in his hold, Mary wrenched herself free.

"Hello Mary."

"It's Miss Heron to you!" spat an outraged Mary.

He chuckled and shook his head, clearly unperturbed by her outburst and smiled that awful, yet charming, half-smile that never failed to turn her insides to mush.

"Ahh, little flower, we both know that's not true."

Anger and indignation rose to overcome the nostalgia and longing that simple nickname brought back. It was only thanks to years of being taught how to compose and ignore her emotions that kept her from exploding at the devilishly handsome man in front of her.

"Do not call me that, my lord." Mary was very proud of herself when her voice came out cold and unfazed.

Alexander Matthews, the seventh Duke of Henwood looked down at the blonde-haired beauty in front of him and stifled a sigh. He wondered if she'd always hate him, and if he'd forever regret leaving her to follow his father's orders. Despite his sober thoughts, Alexander was not one to let the opportunity to vex his little flower go, as that is what she was to him regardless of her feelings over the nickname. Leaning in close and relishing in her little intake of breath, he murmured, "You'll always be my little flower, Marigold."

Mary, who due to his nearness, was trying to keep the butterflies in her stomach calm, barely had time to react to his words before he turned and strode down the corridor, leaving Mary to stare after him in a mixture of annoyance and longing. *Insufferable man,* thought Mary, as she too turned and headed down the corridor, although in a different direction to the one the now smiling man had just gone.

# Chapter Two

## 2 March 1813, London

Strolling through Oxford Street with her best friend, Mary tried to contain her loud, carefree laughter. It had been over a week since her run-in with the devil himself and she hadn't seen hide nor hair of him. . Much to her surprise she only felt disappointment over his absence, so she was trying to take her mind off of him by shopping for ribbons and bonnets with Alice West, the daughter of the Earl of Rutland. They'd only known each other for a few years since they'd both come out in society together, but it felt like they had known each other all of their lives. The day they had met, they had just clicked. It may have been helped by the fact that Alice had needed saving from an overzealous suitor so Mary had stepped in and they'd become instant friends.

Alice was a lot like Mary, slightly shy but fiercely protective of her friends and uncaring over what anyone thought of her. The only difference between the two was their appearance, as where Mary was fair with green eyes and blonde hair, Alice was dark with brown, silky hair and dark eyes. In short, she was beautiful, although Alice would never think of herself as such.

With their maids sitting together on a bench at the entrance of the park, Mary and Alice were free to gossip and talk about their lives without fearing the servants repeating it. The conversation at present was a fine example of this:

"I'm serious, Mary, you should have been there. He squealed like a little girl and it was only a little mouse!" Alice was retelling the story of her and her recent suitor's promenade into Hyde Park the previous afternoon.

"If I'd have been there, you wouldn't have been with him. You're courting, remember? Friends are not usually invited to such outings."

Her friend snorted and waved away her response.

"That hardly signifies. He was so put off by the little animal that he made us leave and returned me home. We'd only just walked in, Mary!"

Her friend was obviously put out by the experience. Alice loved flowers almost as much as Mary did.

"It's okay Alice, we are here now, are we not?"

Alice brightened a little as she surveyed their surroundings, "Yes, yes we are."

The two ladies strolled for a while longer until they heard a deep voice greet them from behind. Mary and Alice turned to find the Viscount of Riverdale, the one who had spoken, and The Duke of Henwood behind them.

Mary felt her eyes widen when she noticed that Alexander the Duke was already staring at her intently. Both Mary and Alice murmured a "my lord" and curtsied as both the gentleman bowed and enquired about their health.

Uncomfortable under his gaze, Mary turned from Alexander and addressed Viscount Riverdale. Always cheerful and pleasant, Mary asked him if he had enjoyed the Viscount Halton's ball this past Friday – the same ball where she and Alexander had spoken. Noticing that his friend was still staring at Miss Heron, and how the lady in question was squirming under his gaze, Ethan Moorwood, more commonly known as the Viscount of Riverdale, decided to cause a little bit of tension for his uptight and too serious a friend.

"Yes, Miss Heron, I did. The ball was very enlightening. Did I see you dancing with the Earl of Hallamshire?" He smiled inwardly at the stiffening of his friend's shoulders and the tinge of red in the lady in question's cheeks.

Ethan waited for Miss Heron's response.

"Err, yes, my lord. I was dancing with him. He is a friend of the family."

Nodding his head, Ethan decided not to push his luck if he wanted his plan to work. "Miss West, did you enjoy yourself at the ball?" he turned towards Alice.

Mary let out a breath when His Lordship addressed Alice. She was unsure of how she felt to have people of the Ton mentioning that she had been dancing with the Earl of Hallamshire, especially when he had been paying calls to their house over the past week. He had yet to ask her father for permission to court Mary, but she knew it was only a matter of time. Sighing, Mary applied her concentration back into the conversation to hear the Viscount teasing Alice over her previous encounter with a certain gentleman and a mouse.

"Walked into anyone else in a darkened corridor recently, little flower?"

Jerking her head at the whispered words, Mary shot a look at the man beside her – the man who had her senses going crazy with only a handful of words. Indignation and the memory of his leaving her, though, kept her back straight.

"I told you not to call me that," hissed Mary, being careful not to let the giggling twosome next to them hear her being so insolent. After all, childhood friend or not, Alexander was still a duke.

"You didn't answer my question."

Mary would never know that by not answering his question, it set his nerves on edge.

"I don't have to. You're not my keeper."

Mary did not consider herself a nasty or rude person, in fact, she was the complete opposite, but this man tended to bring out the worst in her. And telling him that she'd been too afraid of running into him that she hadn't strayed from her mother's side at any balls she'd attended in this past week was out of the question.

Gathering all of his patience, Alexander grit his teeth and asked again whether or not she'd had any potentially ruinous run-ins with other gentlemen.

Hearing the annoyance in his voice and knowing that he too could be mean, Mary sighed and whispered her answer, still conscious of the couple next to them.

"No. No, I haven't."

Letting out the breath he had been holding, Alexander felt himself relax.

"Mary, I—" whatever Alexander had been about to say, Mary would not find out, for Alice and the Viscount had finished their conversation and were now staring at them expectantly.

The foursome chatted about meaningless subjects for a while until the Viscount turned to both Mary and Alice saying they had to be off for another engagement and bid them goodbye, as did the Duke. Bowing to the ladies, the Viscount and Duke turned and strolled away, not noticing how all the women in the park stopped to stare after them, both tall and dark, and clad in form fitting breeches and well-tailored coats, the two men were definitely a sight for sore eyes.

Turning, Mary saw the cheeky grin on her friend's face and just knew she was not going to like what Alice had to say. She was right.

"Was it just me or was there some tension between you and the Duke?"

Not wanting to lie to her friend, but also not sure if there really was tension between them, Mary just shrugged and suggested they go for an ice at the parlour down the street. Alice was aware that her friend was changing the subject, but she trusted her to tell her what was going on between herself and the handsome duke when she was ready. It also helped that sweets were Alice's favourite, especially ice… So she let the subject drop and linked her arm through her best friend's.

Collecting their maids, the two ladies walked arm in arm down the path towards their destination, not caring that being arm in arm with another woman was not acceptable in polite society, and especially not in a place as public as Hyde Park. However, the ladies were not exactly what you would call conventional.

# Chapter Three

## 3 March 1813, London

At 2 pm the next day, Mary's fears were confirmed. The Earl of Hallamshire had asked her father to court her, and her father had said yes.

"Papa please, he's older than you."

"I'm sorry, Mary. He'll provide for you; you are three and twenty, darling. Do you not think you should be grateful that an earl, even an old one as such as Hallamshire, is paying you attention?"

Mary knew then that her father would be of no use. Sighing, she left, reflecting that even though her father loved all of his children and was a kind man, he had always been more interested in his flowers than he had in his children; one of which was now happily married and the other was currently in Rome, soaking up the sun. It was only Mary left in the house that needed to find a husband. She tried a different tactic with her mother, "He's not a nice man, Mama. He touches me inappropriately when we dance."

Her mother looked up from tending to the menus in her office to gaze at her youngest child. Noticing the frustration there, Olivia wondered what was going on behind those green eyes, and if her daughter knew how beautiful she actually was?

"While I do not agree with the inappropriate touching, at least this means he will be able to function if it came to that."

At her mother's blunt words, Mary felt her cheeks flood with colour. Embarrassed, she let out a low splutter, "Mother!" and flopped into the wingback chair in front of her. She covered her face with her hands. Obviously her parents were not going to be of use in this situation, she'd now have to find her own way to discourage the earl.

Trying to make her daughter feel better, Olivia told her that as the earl was old, it was likely that he would die sooner rather than later and that she would be an independent widow in the near future if they married. This only served to make Mary more embarrassed, leading her to concede to a ride in the park with the earl the next day just to get her mother to stop talking.

Forcing herself to smile at her mother, Mary then fled to the library on the east side of the house; a room that never failed to calm her, with walls and walls of books, from ceiling to floor; a large stone fireplace that had been lit and was currently filling the already sunny room with a pleasant warmth. Mary loved it here. She found the book she had left on the table beside one of the oversized chairs earlier that morning before her father had called her into his office to tell her the news, and settled in by the fire and read till the sun went down, losing herself in a world of romance, drama and intrigue.

"I'm so glad you could join me, Miss Heron, it's a pleasure to have you at my side."

Mary kept her polite smile in place and murmured a thank you; she had hoped that the earl would not call this morning but he had. At 12 sharp, there had been a knock on the door, and Mary had been ushered out of the house on the earl's arm, right in front of two of the Ton's biggest gossips, Mrs Wellington and Mrs Beachum. Mary was certain that the whole of the Ton would know that the earl was courting her within the hour. Sighing, Mary turned to the earl and enquired about his health. There was no use being rude to him, as she couldn't change what was happening, and after spending hours the night before trying to come up with a solution, Mary was still no closer to one.

"Are you enjoying your season, Miss Heron?"

"Yes, Your Lordship, I always enjoy being in London. Although I do miss being at home with my dog."

The earl nodded and looked thoughtful, "Oh yes, you have that mutt, do you not?"

Stifling her anger at the earl calling her beloved Percy a bloodhound who had adorably droopy ears and was more often than not tripping over said ears, she replied, "Yes, I have a bloodhound, my lord."

Nodding his head and not realizing his error, the earl continued to talk about mundane topics.

Mary was never happier to see her house when they at last returned. Mary was handed down from the curricle by the earl; he placed a kiss on her knuckles and bade her a good day. Mary curtsied and hoped that the lingering brush of his hand against her side as she walked away was an accident. Unfortunately, Mary knew that was not the case.

# Chapter Four

### 17 March 1813, London

Two weeks. It had been two weeks since the Earl of Hallamshire had officially started courting his little flower, and Alexander was going insane. Watching her now, dancing with the earl for the second time tonight, Alexander could feel his ire and despair rising. For two weeks he had watched Mary dance, laugh, go for rides at the Hyde Park and have ice at the local parlour. Alexander hadn't intentionally meant to see her most of the time, in fact, he tried to ignore her when he could as watching his little flower smile and laugh with another man was not his idea of fun.

He had not spoken to Mary since the incident in the corridor over a month ago and it was getting to him. It did not help that he was currently watching her flirt with a sleaze of a man, a man whose hand had just moved dangerously low on Mary's back. Alexander stepped forward to go wrench the bilious earl's hand from his little flower's body, when he felt a hand on his arm.

"Careful there, old chap, you're scaring the ladies with that thunderous stare of yours."

Ethan, seeing the direction of his friend's gaze and the expression on his face decided to step in before his friend maimed the Earl of Hallamshire. He'd never known his silent and composed best friend to ever lose control over his emotions but apparently, when it came to Miss Heron the rules went out of the window. Suppressing a laugh, Ethan nudged his friend who was still yet to let up his murderous stare.

Looking around at the weary glances the ladies were, in fact, sending his way, Alexander snorted and tugged his arm free of his friends hold.

"Good. Perhaps then they will leave me alone."

Much to Alexander's annoyance, his tone was met with laughter and a slap on the back from his friend.

"Ah yes, that way you will have more time to stare moodily at your Miss Heron."

"She is not my Miss Heron, Ethan."

Amused and unperturbed by his friend's sharp reply, Ethan grinned, and ever insolent, told his dear friend that maybe he should tell himself that, as his eyes had still not left the woman in question.

"She could've been, but not anymore."

Alexander's quiet words surprised and confused Ethan.

"Why not? You obviously care for her."

Ethan was not prepared for the pain and self-hatred he saw in his friend's eyes.

"Because I left her."

With that, Ethan watched his friend storm away and out into the garden, and then he saw the object of his friend's affection sigh longingly as she too noticed Alexander leave.

Mary's heart squeezed as she watched Alexander leave. Sighing with the longing she felt but could do nothing about, Mary turned back to her mother and the Earl of Hallamshire, and prayed that the earl would leave shortly so she could relax her guard. The past two weeks had been torture, not only because the earl had all but given up pretending that he was a gentleman and touched her inappropriately whenever he could. Mary had tried talking to her mother about his unwanted advances and had received "Don't worry darling, he's old, and chances are he's too old to do anything more than touch" in return, something which had both confused and terrified Mary.

It was clear to her that the earl intended to make her his countess, not because he had asked her father for her hand but because he'd constantly refer to her as his, or he'd tell her that when she was his she would not be able to escape him. Mary had stayed away from him as much as she could for the past week, feigning headaches, head colds, and even a stomach ache when she was feeling particularly uncomfortable in the earl's presence. It had not worked, and if anything, her absence and inattention to the earl had made him more determined to see and touch her.

It made Mary uncomfortable and scared over what would happen if he did marry her, and then there was Alexander. Oh how she missed him; they'd been really close as children and romance had blossomed between them very early on. Neither had admitted it to the other, of course, and then he'd been gone and she didn't see him for seven years. Seven years without him after meeting him every day since she was five years old and he was ten. Mary had been sixteen when he had disappeared and to this day she had no idea where he'd gone, only that he hadn't come back till now.

Shrugging away the dark mood that had passed over her, Mary feigned the need for some air and, after declining the earl's offer of assistance, walked out onto the terrace. Gripping the rail in front of her, Mary breathed in deeply. She smelt the flowers and instantly felt herself calm down. Mary had always loved flowers, one of the only traits she'd gotten from her father; they calmed her, and right now Mary would love nothing more than to be at home tending to her own garden, or being at her sister Violet, who currently lived in Scotland, tending to their beautiful and vast garden.

"Mary."

Mary wasn't surprised to hear his voice. He seemed to be everywhere she was these past few weeks. It was part of the reason that the earl's advances were so hard for Mary to accept; the man was also quite a lot older than her but that wasn't exactly unheard of in society. How could Mary accept the earl's advances when she desperately wanted the man standing so close behind her that she could feel the heat of his body soaking into her bones? Mary bathed in the feeling of being surrounded by him and his heat before composing her face into a polite smile and turning to face Alexander.

"What are you doing out here, my lord?" She sounded tired, perhaps she was just tired of fighting her feelings for this man, the man who had left her for seven years. With that thought running through her mind, Mary steeled herself for his reply.

"I was getting some air. I could ask you what you are doing out her all by yourself. You looked very cosy to me not ten minutes ago, dancing with the Earl of Hallamshire."

The venom in his tone surprised Mary.

Alexander had always been guarded when it came to his emotions, yet it was the accusation in his tone that prompted Mary's next words.

"You sound angry, my lord."

"Of course I'm angry! You let that odious man put his hands all over you."

Thankfully they were far enough from the ballroom that they could not be seen and the noise of the music drowned out Alexander's roar as his emotions took a hold of him.

Mary was so surprised to hear Alexander shout as he never had in her presence before, that she didn't even take note of his words for several seconds. Too preoccupied with the fact that he never shouted, his stare did the talking for him; stony and cold, many were scared of him. His words and subsequent anger penetrated Mary's confused brain and stood to fuel her own anger at the audacity of the man.

"He didn't put his hands all over me. Don't be absurd, Alexander. And even if he had, what business is it of yours? It's my body, I can let whomever I want touch me it has nothing to do wi—"

Mary was unable to finish her lie as Alexander's lips crashed down on her own, scattering her thoughts and causing her to forget all about the persistent advances of the earl's. She focused only on the surprisingly soft lips of Alexander Matthew's, the man she had dreamed about for years.

His kiss was hard and unforgiving, as both Mary and Alexander poured their unresolved feelings into the kiss. Mary gasped at the feel of Alexander's hand brushing against her left breast, unlike the earl's touch, Alexander's touch left her weak and wanting more. Alexander took the opportunity of her open mouth to plunge his tongue into hers and explore her warm wetness. The warmth of her mouth on his was dizzying, the feel of her breast in his palm, even over her clothing, was heaven. Alexander groaned, imagining her bare against him and deepened the kiss, his hands roaming over ever part of Mary he could. The span of her small waist, the delicate slope of her shoulders, the slight roundness to her hips, he was about to delve further down her bodice when a loud bang from the ballroom brought them both crashing back to reality. Both gasped for breath and Alexander reluctantly released Mary from his tight hold, fervently hoping that he hadn't bruised her in his wish to have her as close to him as possible.

Alexander cursed himself. He felt like a fool for not controlling himself; a woman like Mary wasn't someone who you grab at in the darkened corner of a terrace.

"Mary I—"

"Don't. Don't you dare apologise for that."

Hand over her mouth, Mary's eyes filled with tears at the regret she saw in his eyes. She had to leave. Turning, she ran blindly down the darkened terrace with tears streaming down her face and found a door leading to a deserted corridor. Mary ran until she found a retiring room where she could regain her composure.

Back on the terrace Alexander starred after Mary. Her tears tore him apart. He shouldn't have kissed her, it was stupid and fuelled by jealousy but regardless of what his little flower thought, he would never apologise for that kiss. Something so amazing could never be wrong, especially not with her. Running a frustrated hand through his hair, Alexander straightened his appearance as best he could in the dark and walked further into the garden so he could sneak away without seeing Mary again, because if he did he'd probably finish what they had started only minutes ago. Lord knew if he did that then he'd have to marry her, and he knew she wouldn't want that, their passionate kiss notwithstanding.

# Chapter Five

## Later That Evening. London, 1813

After righting her appearance and splashing her face with water multiple times in order to reduce the redness from her bout of tears, Mary walked back to the ballroom, her eyes automatically scanning the room for Alexander. He wasn't there and she didn't know if she was happy or disappointed by this fact, however, Mary suspected it was the latter.

Spotting Alice standing across the ballroom conversing with a man who had his back to Mary, she decided to seek refuge with her friend and her companion. It wasn't until Alice had spotted Mary coming towards her that Mary realised who the gentleman was.

"Miss Heron, how lovely to see you again."

Looking into the smiling eyes of the Viscount of Riverdale, Mary smiled back and greeted him. "Hello, my lord. The pleasure is mine."

"Mary, His Lordship and I were just discussing the theft at the Brooks' ball last night. Apparently, they took Mrs Brooks' diamonds and now a twenty pound reward has been issued for anyone who can either return the diamonds or capture the thief."

Mary noticed the slight tensing of the Viscount's shoulders at the mention of finding the thief but thought nothing of it. Turning to view her friend's excited face, Mary felt a little better.

"I did not realise that there had been an incident at the Brooks' last night."

Her friend laughed. "Well you wouldn't, would you Mary? You've been so busy avoiding the earl these past few weeks that I'm surprised you've noticed anything at all."

Colouring at her friend's statement, Mary looked at the Viscount to see what his reaction to her avoiding one of his set would be, only to find him grinning at her.

"Ah, but Miss West, we both know that if we were being courted by the Earl of Hallamshire, we'd both hide away from his advances."

Alice looked thoughtful for a minute until she threw the Viscount a teasing grin.

"Why, my lord, I think you may be right."

The earl's loud laughter greeted her statement, causing a few heads to turn in their direction, not that the threesome noticed.

Mary spent the rest of the evening with the Ethan and Alice letting their playful conversation and laughter flow over her and help sooth her frayed emotions that had been tested over the course of the evening. First by the Earl of Hallamshire and then by Alexander. Mary didn't let herself think of the kiss they had shared until that evening, she could still feel his hands on her skin, his mouth on hers, the regret in his eyes.

# Chapter Six

### 23 March 1813, London

It was of no use; she was not going to be able to get him out of her head. Throwing her book to the side in frustration, Mary rose and walked to the window, angrily swiping at her waist length hair that she'd lazily left unbound after her bath earlier in the evening. She hadn't seen Alexander for days, she'd looked for him at every ball but had yet to lay her eyes on him. Watching the rain fall down in torrents. Mary felt a certain sense of companionship with the weather. It suited her temperament; all dark and stormy. Mary was unaware that her life was about to become much more complicated than simply dealing with an elusive duke.

"Mary, darling, I have some news."

She looked at her father as he walked through the door and sat in one of the chairs by the fire. As he gestured for her to sit, Mary could see the solemn look on her father's face and wondered what was wrong. Taking a seat, Mary folded her hands in her lap and waited for her father to speak.

"Mary, I… I am not sure how to tell you this."

Mary could feel butterflies going wild in her stomach and her mind was racing; her father was never one to mince his words and had never been stuck for how to tell someone something. *Had someone seen me and Alexander the week before, am I ruined, wha—*

"The earl has asked permission to marry you."

Stunned into silence, Mary could only stare in horror at her father. This could not be happening, she knew the earl wanted to make her his countess but she never thought it would happen so quickly. Couples courted for months before any offer was made, and it had only been a few weeks; this was a disaster.

"I know you do not want to marry the earl so I asked him for some time to think the situation over before giving him my permission. Do not worry my darling girl, if you cannot reconcile yourself to marry him then you have no need to. I will not force you, and neither will your mother."

Looking at the honesty in her father's eyes, Mary felt slightly less like the sky was caving in.

"Thank you, Papa, but we both know if I was to snub the earl, I'd lose all hope of finding a good match."

Her father sighed and reached over to squeeze his daughter's hand.

She looked so lost and forlorn, he knew she did not want to marry the earl, hell he did not want his daughter to marry the earl, but his daughter was right. If she was to refuse the earl, even as old and unsuited to her as he was, her chances of finding a good match would dwindle. Not that anyone would blame her for refusing the earl but there would be whispers about her. He didn't want that for his little girl.

Squeezing her hand again, he offered something that he hoped would make his daughter a little happier.

"I suggested to the earl that if he were to court you for a while longer, you would be more likely to say yes and therefore would save him the embarrassment of a rejection. He was furious over my proposal but he agreed nonetheless."

Letting go of his daughter's hand, Edwin Heron hoped that his daughter would be happy with the earl when the time came.

"It'll be okay, Mary."

Once her father had left, Mary let the tears fall that she'd felt welling up from the moment her father had told her the news. She felt trapped and couldn't see a way out. Bless her father for giving her an extra week to ready herself for a life with the earl. Covering her face, Mary let the sobs out. Up until ten minutes ago, she'd only had her conflicting feelings for Alexander to work through and now she had a life of marriage to a man, whose touch turned her stomach. Oh how was she going to get out of this, and what was Alexander going to say when he found out? Nothing, he'd say nothing, as their kiss had been a mistake; he knew it and so did she. No. Mary knew he cared for her, maybe not the way she cared for him, but he cared for her nonetheless. Wiping the tears from her face, Mary replaced her book on the shelf and carried her weary body off to bed. There was nothing she could do to change her situation tonight.

# Chapter Seven

## 27 March 1813, White's Gentlemen Club. London

Alexander was sitting at White's, staring into his scotch and thinking about a certain lady when Ethan sat down next to him. The Viscount had been watching his friend stare at his drink for the past ten minutes and had realised that his friend's mind was far away. Ethan was not looking forward to telling his friend what he had just found out, he knew Alexander was going to react badly.

"A penny for them."

Alexander started at his friend's voice. Shrugging out of his thoughts Alexander smiled at Ethan, the man who had befriended him when he'd come to London alone and new to his dukedom.

"They are worth much more than that." Shooting his friend a grin, Alexander felt himself relax and was released from his dark thoughts from minutes ago and took a sip of his drink. He felt the burn of the liquid as it slid down his throat. "Did you hear about the Earl of Hallamshire?" Alexander felt himself tense at the mention of that man's name and wondered what his friend was about to tell him. Alexander hoped that it was that the earl had died in his sleep. Unfortunately, Alexander did not get his wish. Rather, Ethan's next words set his world on fire.

"There's a rumour going around that he's asked the Earl of Winchcombeshire for his daughter's hand in marriage."

"What?" Alexander's shout in the quiet of White's earned them some looks but once they saw the furious look on the Duke's face everyone quickly turned away, wondering what the Viscount could have said to anger the usually composed Duke.

"What?" repeating himself, albeit a few decibels lower than his previous outburst, Alexander felt his mind racing. She couldn't marry the earl; she was his, she'd kissed him back, he knew she had. This couldn't be happening.

"Yes, the news has been going around for the past few days."

"And you're only telling me now?" The accusation in Alexander's voice did not faze Ethan. If he had been in his friend's shoes, he would have been just as angry.

"I only found out tonight. It seems your Miss Heron has been avoiding all outings for the past four days. Apparently her father asked the earl for a week to let Miss Heron get used to the idea."

Alexander quickly worked out that if the earl had spoken to Mary's father four days ago then Mary only had three days until she would have to give her answer to the earl, because while no one would blame his little flower for refusing the earl it would brand her as a picky spinster at three and twenty. Mary was considered on the shelf by many of the ton. Ridiculous, he knew, but that was the way of things.

Alexander had to see her, he had to find out if she wanted to marry the earl. If she did he would leave her alone, he would not force her to be with him if she did not want to. Shocked at the direction of his thought's Alexander took another large sip of his drink. He did not want to get married, and certainly not to Mary, the one woman who had held his heart for years. The only woman who could also crush him with her rejection.

Shaking his head, Alexander pushed his feelings of fear aside.

"Where is she?" he demanded of his friend but Alexander didn't care that he was being rude to his good friend. He knew Ethan would forgive him and he had to find her.

"She's at the Fallon's ball. It's the first one she has attended all week."

Alexander didn't hear his friend wish him luck or his happy laughter as he was already out of his seat and striding towards the door; seeing Mary, the only thing on his mind.

# Chapter Eight

### That Same Night, Just Before Our Hero Finds out About a Certain Impending Engagement, London

"There's been another theft, this time at the Vancouver's ball two nights ago. They say the thief stole emeralds this time." Barely listening to her friend's retelling of the balls she had missed over the last four days, Mary was in a state of despair.

It had been four days since her father had told Mary of the earl's proposal and she had been in hiding ever since, she knew that the news of the earl's conversation with her father would get out and had feared Alexander's reaction, or, his non-reaction. That fear was enough to keep herself hidden away, and it was a good way to keep herself from having to see the earl. Not an hour since Mary had overheard some of the younger ladies discussing her and the earl, they had wondered harshly why someone so plain and as firmly on the shelf as Mary was the object of the wealthy earl's affection? Obviously they weren't perturbed by the earl's age. His wealth, Mary suspected, was enough to make them forget the earl's advanced years.

"Don't look now but there is a very angry duke striding towards us."

Watching her friend's eyes widen in alarm, Mary felt her own gut tighten in response as she knew which duke her friend was referring to. He was here, and seeing him now, she judged from the look of the fire in his eyes that he knew.

"Miss West, would you mind terribly if I stole Miss Heron away for a turnabout the room?"

Both ladies knew by the tone of his voice that he was not going to take no for an answer, Mary felt herself bristle at his tone. She had not seen him since their kiss and his anger with her now did not help endear him to her.

"And if I mind, my lord?" Standing straight and meeting his gaze, Mary felt her ire fading when she saw the conflicting emotions in his eyes.

"Do you?" his murmured words sought to dissolve the last of her ire.

"No." Stifling a sigh, Mary placed her hand on his arm and let him lead her to the side of the dance floor.

For a full tensed minute neither of them spoke. Mary knew she would cave under the pressure soon so was grateful when Alexander broke the silence.

"So, you are to marry the earl."

Mary was surprised, not only because she hadn't expected Alexander to mention her impending engagement but also because he hadn't called her his little flower, which, even though she protested whenever he did, disappointed her as she secretly loved his nickname for her.

"Nothing is confirmed yet, my lord."

Deciding that if he was going to treat her as if they had never been friends then she would do the same. Neither said anything as they passed by the chaperone bench, not wanting anyone to know what they were discussing. Alexander's furious face as he walked in, had already set the gossip mill churning, with many of the guests turning to glance at the dancing couple more than once. .

Once they'd passed the chaperone bench Alexander took advantage of a commotion happening at the other end of the ball room and led Mary out into a corridor and into what looked like a music room. While Alexander wasn't aware that there was to be music this evening he wasn't surprised as he had been so intent on seeing Mary, that he had paid little attention to what was happening at the gathering tonight.

Candles had been placed around the room, casting a soft glow over the room. Alexander released Mary to run his hands through his hair, he had not thought that he was going to do once he got her alone, just that he had to. Pushing the door part way closed to give them some privacy, Alexander turned to Mary and felt all his anger over the situation disappear. He couldn't be mad at her when she looked so lost, and so damn sad.

"Do you want to marry him?" he asked.

Looking at Alexander, Mary realized she couldn't lie to him. She could say that yes, she wanted to marry the earl and he would let her; she could see it in his eyes, she could see that he would ignore the kiss they'd shared and any feelings he may or may not have for her.

Mary shook her head sadly, "No, no I do not wish to marry him, but I have no choice. We both know that no one would have me if I don't. I'd be branded a spinster more than I already am."

Mary turned from him. It was too hard to tell him that she had to marry another man when he was looking at her so intently. Those blue eyes of his were like magnets, it was difficult for Mary to drag her eyes away. "The earl, he would be good to me, and I'd want for nothing. I'm lucky he's even interested, I'm three and twenty! And I'm certainly nothing special."

Mary felt herself being spun around as the last words slipped unbidden from her mouth.

"You are special. You are beautiful and never let anyone convince you otherwise."

Alexander shook her for good measure and Mary could see the fire and truth in his eyes and felt her own fill with tears. She hated this, hated that she would soon be engaged to a man she who made her feel physically ill, all because the Ton would shun her. She was the daughter of an earl. It was silly that she would be treated so poorly all because she didn't want to marry a man three times older than herself.

"Oh little flower, what are we going to do?"

Alexander's hushed question came as a surprise.

Mary hadn't realised that Alexander was still holding her, hadn't realised that his face was still so close to hers. Mary realised then that she could have this man if it wasn't for the earl, and his leaving her all those years ago, Alexander could've been hers.

"I don't know, I really don't know Alexander."

Feeling as lost and confused as she did, Mary was bewildered to see Alexander smile. The confusion must have shown on her face for Alexander squeezed her shoulders and pulled her closer.

"You called me Alexander, you haven't done so since our kiss."

His words lit a fire in Mary's stomach, images of his hands on her, his mouth on her skin heated her entire body. His words must have had the same effect on Alexander for he leaned down and pressed his lips to Mary's just as the door was pushed opened and a gasp spread through the room.

# Chapter Nine

## 27 April 1813, London

"My lord, what are you doing?"

At the sound of Mrs Wellington voice, Mary knew she was ruined. News of her kiss with Alexander would be all over the ballroom within minutes of Mrs Wellington leaving. Alexander still had a hold of her shoulders; he had frozen at the sound of Mrs Wellington's shrill words. Breaking free of his hold Mary turned to face the door and found three pairs of eyes staring at her. It was worse than she thought as accompanying Mrs Wellington were Mrs Beachum and Mrs Webster. Mary inwardly groaned; out of everyone who could have come across them, the three ladies standing in front of her were the absolute worst. Mrs Webster pressed her hands to her face in horror. Mary thought the move overly dramatic but she refrained from saying so, as she understood the severity of the situation she had put herself in.

"She's ruined; she'll never be accepted into polite society again."

Mary felt herself bristle at the mention of her ruination, it was absurd that the Duke of Henwood would marry her, while her breeding was impeccable, and as the daughter of an earl, she had more than an ample dowry, but Mary was old by ton's standards and therefore, not suitable for a duke of Alexander's standing.

"No."

Mary looked sympathetically at Alexander; she knew he must believe that he had to marry her in order to save her reputation, Alexander was like that. The ton would never blame him if he refused to marry her, and no one wanted to be forced into marriage. And Mary would not make him sacrifice his happiness to save her reputation.

Stealing herself for what she was about to say, Mary looked to the floor and said, “My lord, it’s okay. I can go and live with my sister in Scotland. It wouldn’t be a problem. I love my sister and they have an amazing garden, and my parents wouldn’t miss me when I’m gone.”

Fingers underneath her chin dragged her gaze back to Alexander, he was looking at her like she had gone insane in the last five minutes since he’d kissed her.

“I’d miss you, and my name is Alexander little flower, you’ve used it before, and you will not being going to Scotland.”

Ignoring his gentle tone and comforting words, Mary knew she had to disagree with him.

“But, my lord, I have to. I cannot stay, not after this.”

“The girl is right, my lord, she cannot stay now that she is ruined, no one would accept her.”

The look Alexander gave Mrs Beachum accentuated his order for her to be quiet.

“She will stay, especially since she has just agreed to marry me before you rudely barged in. Now if you will excuse us, I’d like to have a few quiet words with my fiancé.”

Ushering the ladies to the door, and closing it firmly behind them, Alexander turned to find Mary staring at him in shock.

“You—” Mary paused and tried to get her thoughts in order. “But you can’t marry me!”

“I can and I am.”

Alexander’s tone left no room for Mary to argue so she just looked at him in disbelief.

“Mary I know you do not want to marry me but it has to be done. Do not worry, I will be a good husband. I hope you will not hate me forever, just remember we were friends before.”

Too worried over her potential rejection Alexander talked quickly and did not give Mary a chance to disagree with him.

"I will call on you tomorrow and speak with your mother and father about the details of our wedding." Taking Mary's hand, he delivered her back to her mother, informed her mother of his plans, kissed Mary's hand and bid them both goodbye.

Whistling a little tune as he left, Alexander reflected on what had just happened. He did not like that Mary had been subjected to those gossiping women's criticism, but he could not fault his good fortune.

Alexander could hear his father orders to stay away from Mary in his mind but, after spending time with Mary and realising what he had been missing out on for all those wasted years, he no longer cared. He smiled at the thought; he was to marry his little flower and Alexander could not see a problem with that, his fear of her rejection notwithstanding.

# Chapter Ten

## 28 March 1813, London

As promised, Alexander called upon them the next day. Their wedding was set to take place in two weeks. Her mother was not pleased, but then again, neither was Alexander, for he had originally intended to marry Mary within the week. The countess had refused outright stating that the scandal would be too great if they were to marry so quickly. She was also unconvinced that she would be able to plan her daughter's wedding within the time frame she was given but she agreed, for Alexander would not relent to pushing the wedding even further back.

Alexander had pointed out that what had happened in the music room at the Fallon's ball had been fodder for the sharks of the town for the past twenty-four hours and had already been retold and exaggerated. The scandal was already great, especially since it involved Alexander. The countess had not appreciated Alexander's observation but had ultimately relented when it was pointed out that his name would protect Mary more than a lengthy engagement. Alexander was to obtain a special licence and the countess was given two weeks to plan their wedding.

Mary's parents had thought it best if Alexander waited until the following day to see Mary as she was still adjusting to the situation. Alexander protested, for he wanted nothing more than to see Mary but from the look on her parents' faces he knew there was no reason to argue. So he left and promised to return the next day to take Mary riding in the park, all the while hoping to catch a glimpse of her as he left.

# Chapter Eleven

### 29 March 1813, London

The following day Mary was awaiting Alexander's promised visit when their butler Avery announced the Earl of Hallamshire.

"Hello, Miss Heron, it's lovely to see you again."

The sneer on the earl's face told Mary it was anything but. However, Mary thought it pertinent to be polite to the man she had technically just rejected.

"My lord, please have a seat while I ring for tea."

Once she had told the maid to prepare them a pot of tea and biscuits, Mary turned to walk to the chair at the far side of the room. It was also the furthest away from the sneering earl. Mary hesitated when the earl blocked the path to her chair.

"Please sit, my lord, the maid will only be a moment." She gave the earl a hesitant smile. Mary tried to move around the earl but he did not give her way…

"No, I don't think I will, my sweet fiancée," the earl gave her a cruel smile and snapped his fingers.

"Oh wait, you're not my fiancée, are you? You are engaged to the Duke of Henwood."

The earl looked straight into Mary's eyes, his were cold and filled with hate.

"I misjudged you, Mary. I was led to believe that you needed time to get used to the idea of marrying me, but it turns out that you just wanted more time to be a whore!"

During his speech the earl had stalked much closer to Mary and fairly roared his last few words. He picked up a strand of Mary's hair that had escaped her braid and tugged.

Hard. Gasping at the pain, Mary took a step back from the earl only to have him take a step towards her. This continued until Mary felt her back press against the wall.

"Please, my lord. I am terribly sorry for what happened but I never agreed to marry you."

"It was understood!" Spit flew from the earl's mouth and onto Mary's face. Mary felt fear crawling along her spine and wondered where the maid was with her tea. Mary hoped she would arrive soon.

"You see, Miss Heron, to have someone such as you humiliate me like that is not acceptable and you will have to pay for that."

Mary was sure he was about to hit her. She closed her eyes and waited for the blow; even Mary knew that the earl would easily overpower her.

"My lord, it would be wise if you were to remove your hands and step away from my daughter."

Obviously the earl was not concerned by her mother's threat as he did not move,

"And why, dear countess, would I do that?"

"Because if you don't, I will not be held responsible for my actions."

Mary's eyes flew to her father's and saw the hatred there. The earl must have heard the danger in her father's voice for he stepped back and released Mary.

"Now be a good sport and remove yourself from my house, Do not come back, for I hear my daughter's fiancé is a brilliant shot and I'm not too bad myself. Here, I'll show you out." Placing his hands on the earl's shoulders, her father escorted him from the room.

"Oh Mary, are you okay?" Rushing to her daughter, Olivia checked to make sure she was unharmed. Once satisfied that her daughter was physically unharmed, Olivia called for the maid. She and her husband had intercepted in the corridor when they had heard the earl's raised voice. Oliva wondered to herself as she poured herself and her daughter a warm cup of tea, how long it would be until the image of her daughter pushed up against the wall by that awful man would leave her mind? Olivia suspected it would be a very long time.

While sipping their tea, neither spoke until Mary's father walked back into the room, after having disposed of the earl.

"Well, at least you are not marrying that man, for I may have had to kill him if you were."

Stunned, Mary could not stop the horrified laugh that escaped her at hearing her father talk about murdering a man. She knew her father would never joke about such things and was therefore very serious. "Mary, he would have hurt you, had your mother and I not arrived in time. I am truly sorry for not listening to you when you said you did not want to marry him."

"It's okay, Papa. I'm not marrying him. I'm marrying Alexander."

Mary was unaware that her face took on a happy glow when she mentioned Alexander but her parents saw it and shared a knowing look.

"You know, Mary, when I heard of the events of the Fallon's ball, I was concerned but I know that the Duke will never hurt you. He may not always be agreeable but he will care for you more strongly than anyone I know. You are, after all, his little flower."

Mary felt her cheeks heat at the mention of Alexander's nickname for her on her father's lips. Her blush just served to make her father grin even more. They, as a family, sat drinking tea and discussing their day until Alexander arrived. To say he was livid about what had happened earlier that day would be an understatement. It took her father, Mary and her mother to reassure him that the earl would no longer bother Mary, for him to momentarily calm down. Later, a rather long, possessive kiss when her parents had left the room served best to dissipate his anger.

Their ride in Hyde Park turned into a sedate walk due to the amount of people milling about, but Mary enjoyed every minute in Alexander's company. Regardless of everything that had happened with the earl this afternoon, Mary went to sleep with a smile on her face and a warmth in her heart that had not been there before.

# Chapter Twelve

## 11 April 1813. A Carriage Somewhere in the South of England

Their wedding was beautiful. In typical London fashion no expense was spared, even for a wedding that had been planned rather quickly. The bride and groom only had eyes for one another, a fact that escaped none of their guests.

For Mary, their wedding passed in a blur of people, bright colours and Alexander. Her husband. Mary pressed a hand to her stomach in an attempt to stop the flutters that erupted at the thought of Alexander being her husband. It was surreal, and she loved it. Looking at the man in question sitting across from her in the carriage, she sighed. He had been amazing these past two weeks, attentive, caring and a constant source of support which Mary supposed was not any different to their past relationship, before he had left. Their journey would take them over two days due to his ancestral home being so far from London, meaning, they would be staying in posting inns for the next two nights.

It was on her second sigh that Alexander laughed, "For a new wife, you are sighing a lot. Should I be worried that I am already failing as a husband?"

The laughter in his tone softened the seriousness of his question and lifted Mary's already high spirits.

"Of course not, dear husband. I was just thinking of the boy you once were."

"Ahh yes, and if I recall little flower, I was a lot better at climbing trees than you were."

His cheeky grin was enough to set Mary's cheeks ablaze, which was of course his intention.

Sticking her nose in the air in an attempt at ignoring him, Mary primly said, "I have no idea what you are referring to, my lord."

"Oh I think you do, little flower."

Mary shrieked at the sound of his voice in her ear. He had somehow managed to cross the carriage and sit beside her without Mary realising it.

"I think you know exactly what I am referring to. Your blush confirms it, my dear wife."

His grin widened at the sight of his wife's flustered spluttering, and Alexander decided to tease his little flower more. He nuzzled his nose into her neck, the same neck that had been driving him crazy for hours. He had seen her hair up plenty of times before but today her neck was especially alluring. Hearing her gasp, an answering smirk settled onto Alexander's lips, the same lips that had stared feathering kisses along the parts of her neck and lower, at the skin not covered by her gown.

"My lord, we are in a carriage!"

Chuckling at her use of his title, and no longer perturbed by it now that she was his, Alexander decided his innocent little wife could not take any more teasing. He still decided to pull her into his lap. Alexander could not say he was not a little aroused by his wife's shriek and pulled her close to his hard form.

"Stop squirming, little flower, unless you want your wedding night to take place in our carriage. I am only a man."

Mary had never stopped moving so quickly in her life, she had had the talk with her mother the previous evening and could feel her cheeks heating at the very memory. She wondered if she would always resemble a tomato around her husband. Alexander's roaring laugh in her ear dragged Mary out of her thoughts. When he had finally calmed down enough to speak, Alexander cleared up some of Mary's obvious confusion, that is, after he had kissed her soundly.

"You make a beautiful tomato, dear wife, so never fear. And I love your blush." He punctuated that sentence by claiming Mary's lips in another brain-numbing kiss.

It was then that Alexander's words registered and Mary realised she had thought her private question aloud, deepening her blush and causing her husband to laugh and kiss her all over again.

Later that night, they stopped and had supper at the posting inn they were to stay at for the night. Once they were settled in their room, Alexander dismissed their servants and spent the rest of the evening showing his new bride the delights of being married and how a little teasing in the right situation was very good, very good indeed.

# Chapter Thirteen

## 8 May 1812, Henwood

The weeks following their wedding were, for Mary, pure bliss. Alexander was attentive, loving, and insatiable. He was always there when she needed him. Although Mary had noticed his withdrawal from her emotionally, it was not that he was any different towards her, but Mary could feel it in the way he looked at her. It was almost as if a barrier came down on his thoughts and feelings. Mary never felt more alone when that happened.

Their days were filled with meeting their tenants, staff and any tasks that were not completed by the horde of servants her husband employed.

Mary was wandering around trying to find the house keeper, Mrs Bisset, when she literally ran into her husband. With his hands around his wife's waist, Alexander breathed in her scent, a mixture of lavender and soap. The scent had driven him mad for years, and he had always wondered how she managed it. He now knew that the lavender came from sprigs she put into her bath, something he found rather charming. Mary was not a woman he would have thought of as having sprigs of lavender in her bath but he was pleasantly surprised that she did. Squeezing her waist, Alexander grinned.

"If you wanted to be in my arms, little flower, all you had to do was ask. You know I love to hold you."

Looking into those blue eyes, Mary could not help but get lost in them.

"Maybe I just like banging into you as I walk around, dear husband."

"Well then, I shall endeavour to make myself available for whenever you would like to bang into me."

Releasing her, Alexander stroked her face.

"Come, I have something to show you."

Grabbing her hand, Alexander practically dragged Mary down the hall in his excitement. It wasn't until Mary was practically jogging to keep up with him, did he give her a sheepish smile and slowed his pace.

When they reached a set of double doors, Alexander instructed Mary to close her eyes. Once Alexander was satisfied Mary was not going to peak, he opened the doors and ushered her in. Closing the doors behind him, he spoke softly to his little flower, "Open your eyes, Mary."

Mary's gasp echoed throughout the large room. Bookshelves, many of which were full, covered almost every inch of the room. Two large floor-to-ceiling windows were the centre point of the room, and served to flood the room with brilliant sunlight. Also, a stone fireplace and two large wingback chairs was centre stage of the wall furthest away. Bookshelves surrounded the fireplace. Mary had never seen anything more beautiful, and Alexander had never seen anything more beautiful than the expression on his wife's face as she took in her surroundings. Awe, surprise, gratitude and another emotion that he did not recognise were all displayed on his little flower's face.

"Do you like it?" He could see from her face that she did but he needed to hear her say it.

"Oh Alexander, it's beautiful, I–I do not know what to say to thank you for showing me this."

Seeing the genuine pleasure on her face Alexander felt a fluttering in his stomach, something that he had never felt before.

"A kiss will suffice, dear wife."

Alexander had taken to calling her his wife more and more, his previous nickname for her was still used more often than not, but it comforted Alexander to remind himself that she was, in fact, now his.

Wrapping her hands around her husband's neck, Mary placed her lips lightly against his, still too shy to indicate anything more substantial. Luckily for Mary, her husband had no such qualms and was quite happy to deepen their kiss, and convince her to go upstairs with him in order to show him just how appreciative she really was.

# Chapter Fourteen

## 13 May 1813, Henwood

Mary was sitting in the library, as was her usual habit, when their butler, James, handed her a letter from what she later found out was her sister. The letter came as a pleasant, and welcome, surprise. Alexander was out for the morning and Mary had nothing to do bar read and wander around the halls. Settling into the wingback chair that Mary had claimed as her own in front of the fire, she began to read her sister's letter.

*My dearest Mary,*

*I cannot believe you are married. I am so happy for you and wish you well and pray that you find as much happiness as I have in my own marriage.*

*When are you bringing Alexander to see me? I don't think I have seen that young man, or I suppose he is no longer a young man. Anyway, I suppose since I have not seen him in over seven years since I left, so I am sure he will not begrudge me my lack of knowledge on your husband's status as a man or boy.*

*Your nephew is beautiful. Angus and I would have named him after a flower to continue father's tradition had he been a girl, but alas, that was not the case. So we settled on Augustus, after many arguments and spoon throwing, that is. It suits him rather well, unfortunately all dear Augustus does at present is sleep. Although as he is very, very pretty so I often find myself watching him sleep.*

*I would not want you to be separated from your darling husband but if you ever feel the need for a spontaneous trip to Scotland then you are always welcome here at Glenalmond.*

*Although it would probably take over a week for you to get here so the longer you plan to stay the better, dear sister.*

*Speaking of spontaneous visits, our dear brother Charles is back. He came to visit a week or so ago and it was wonderful. He is unfashionably tanned but his stories of the colonies and India and Greece are fascinating. Oh Mary, he is grown. I know as the eldest, I often think of you both as the snot riddled babes you once were, but he is a man now. At two and thirty, I know I am not much older than Charles but it is still a shock to see my brother of eight and twenty years, who I may add is the same age as your dashing husband, looking so mature and put together. I am sure when I see you that I will burst into tears over my forgotten youth.*

*I miss you, Marigold. I cannot believe both Charles and I missed your wedding. Please forgive me for that but with the new babe I did not want to travel so far, but that does not mean I am not very happy for you.*

*Oh, the babe must want his mama for he is screaming very loudly. We have nannies and staff to look after him but as you will find out soon enough, there is nothing better than holding that babe in your own arms.*

*I shall stop writing now and attend to Augustus.*

*Love always,*
*Violet Ainsley.*
*Countess of Glenalmond.*

Mary felt her heart swell to know that her sister and brother were both happy. While her brother was not married, Mary knew he enjoyed his life as a traveller. Sighing a happy contented smile, Mary closed her eyes intending on getting up and finding Alexander in a minute or two. Instead Mary fell asleep and was asleep still when Alexander found her hours later.

# Chapter Fifteen

## Later That Afternoon, Henwood

"Do you fancy a walk into the forest today, little flower?" Opening her eyes, Mary glanced at her husband who was sitting in the chair across from her. Mary was not aware that he had found her an hour earlier and had watched her over his scotch until he had seen her eyelids flicker. Straightening from her slouched position, Mary tried to smooth her hair that she was sure would be a mess. "The forest?"

The smile Mary gave him had him moving to her and picking her up in order to rearrange her on his lap in the chair that was still warm from her sleepy body. Seeing the blush on her face made Alexander smile. He vowed to himself that for as long as he lived, he would endeavour to keep her blushing as much as he could.

"Yes, our lands are vast, and since you love books ardently, I wondered if you would like to see what your books look like in their natural state."

Smiling, Alexander cuddled his wife closer and relished in the feel of her soft curves against the hard planes of his own.

Feeling herself relax, Mary breathed deeply, still not very used to the feel of his hands on her.

"That would be lovely. Oh!"

Mary started when she felt Alexander's hands brush lower on her body and when his lips found the sensitive spot behind her ear, Mary knew she was lost.

"You know, wife, I have suddenly thought of another way to spend our afternoon. A much more, satisfying way."

With a laugh, Mary let her husband seduce her in the middle of their library. It was another hour before they made to the forest.

# Chapter Sixteen

## Henwood Forest

"This is all yours?"

Mary looked around her in amazement. She was aware that Alexander's lands were extensive, he was a duke, after all, but she was not aware until now just how extensive they were. The incredulity in his wife's voice made Alexander smile, and that coupled with the blush that had yet to dissipate from their time together in the library brought a warmth to Alexander's heart that he had not expected.

"Ours? This is yours now too, Mary."

Smiling broadly at her husband, Mary continued to look around at their surroundings. The sun was shining brilliantly today, birds were chirping a pleasant tune and Mary even saw a squirrel on their walk. This part of the woods formed almost a walkway, with leaves overhead and all around with big, thick tree trunks in a row on either side of them served to create a barrier of sorts for them to walk through. Tree roots caused ruts that needed slight navigation due to flowers and grass covering them, when Mary tripped, Alexander took her hand and walked with her down the path.

"It's beautiful, Alexander."

Her soft praise made him almost deliriously happy. He had taken refuge in this part of the woods as a young boy and it had always held a special place in his heart. Seeing Mary enjoy and appreciate his sanctuary as much as he did loosened some of the pain he had carried in his heart since he was a very young boy. It really was a beautiful place, though his father had never thought so. The one time Alexander had told him about his sanctuary, his father had scoffed and told him to stop with such notions, and sent him to live with his grandparents the next day. Caught off-guard by the thoughts of his father, Alexander did not realise he had stopped walking until Mary called his name.

"Alexander?"

Confused as to why he had stopped walking, Mary called to him a second time when her first attempt failed to rouse him from whatever thoughts ailed him. This time around he turned those big blue eyes of his on her and she was lost. His eyes had always been her weakness, not his smile, not his charm, but his eyes – those pools of blue that seemed to never end.

"I love you." So lost in his eyes, Mary did not sensor her thoughts and the words were out before she could stop them.

But now that she had said them, she would not take them back. She did love Alexander, had loved him since they were children and he had helped her climb down from a tree after she had gotten stuck and was then too scared to even attempt to climb down alone. Alexander had teased her relentlessly about her resemblance to a flower with her balancing on a tree branch when he came across her and her name, and Mary had been so busy telling him that she was not a flower, nor was she little and to stop calling her Marigold that she was out of the tree and back on the ground before she knew it. He had been her hero and she had been his little flower ever since.

Although looking at him now you would never believe that her hero was the same person as the man standing in front of her, for this man was frozen. Mary was not even sure he was breathing. Since her outburst he had not said anything, just stood there looking at her unblinking.

Unable to stand his stare and silence any longer, Mary whispered his name when minutes went by without him moving.

"Alexander, please say something."

He seemed to blink himself back to life, his face lit up and Mary's heart soared only to crash back down to earth at his next words.

"I can't."

“Can’t what? You can’t love me back?”

He flinched and looked so broken that Mary felt her own heart crack in response. Mary ran from him, left him in a place that was so beautiful minutes ago and now only held pain.

Mary hoped that one day, when his rejection was less fresh she could go back to those trees and find the beauty in them again.

But not now, now she had to leave. She knew that he had only married her to save her but she had thought in the last few weeks that he had come to care for her as more than a childhood friend. Mary was not prepared for his rejection.

On her sprint back to the house Mary decided that she could not stay while his rejection was so fresh, she would go to her sister’s for a few weeks and come back when she could look at him again without seeing his tormented face in her mind’s eye.

Mary knew she would be welcome at her sister’s. It also helped that it would, as her sister had stated, take over a week for Mary to get to her sister’s which meant a lot of time in a carriage and posting inns to give her time to think about what just happened with her marriage. Realising that Alexander would worry, for he did care for her as her friend, Mary made sure to tell their butler that she was going away for a while but would be back in a month or two.

# Chapter Seventeen

## Very Late That Same Night, Henwood

His little flower was gone and it was his fault. When she had run from him Alexander had stayed in the forest until the sun had set. He did not move for hours, could not have moved. He was in shock. He had not expected Mary to confess her love for him. He was not sure why he had not expected it, and they had known each other since they were children. He had been best friends with her brother for nearly two decades, and friends with Mary for just as long, however, their friendship had been more because he found her charming when she would follow him and Charles around, begging to let her play. More often than not they had done so more to get her to stop asking them than anything. For the life of him Alexander did not know why he had said he couldn't in the forest. He would probably never know for he loved her, he always had even when they were children and she had been more child than anything. At first he just felt protective of her until she got stuck in that blasted tree. She had been so furious with him about calling her Marigold, and had never looked more beautiful to him.

Sitting in her chair in the library with his head in his hands, Alexander was at a loss. He did not know where she would be, he did not think she would go back to London but if she wanted to get away from him then maybe she did. Their butler had informed him that Mary had said she would be back in a month or two but alexander could not wait that long to get her back. He just did not know where to look.

Turning at the feel of something digging into his spine, Alexander noticed what looked like a letter stuffed into the chair. Pulling the letter out Alexander began to read what looked like a letter to Mary from her sister. Usually, he would not read his wife's mail but Alexander felt that if it helped him to find his wife then a little rule bending was valid. Glenalmond? Scotland? He knew her sister had married and moved to Scotland but would Mary go there if she felt she could not stay here? Alexander decided it was too big a possibility for him not to go and see her sister. It would take too long for a letter to get there and back, too long of not knowing where his wife was.

James had also told him that his little flower had taken the carriage so he may be able to reduce his travelling time if he went on horseback, it was a crazy idea as it would be a long hard ride to Scotland but he had to get her back. Had to tell her that he did love her, of course he did, she was his, she always had been.

Decision made Alexander strode towards the door and if the clock had not struck eleven pm just as he was about to go fetch a horse, Alexander would have been on his way to find his wife. Instead he went to the kitchen, got himself some leftovers from dinner since he had not eaten since lunch and slept in a guest room for he could not face sleeping in their bed without his little flower snuggled up beside him.

At day break the following morning, Alexander was on his best horse riding off in the direction of Glenalmond. Praying all the while that Mary was okay and that he would not be too late to explain once he found her.

# Chapter Eighteen

## 23 May 1813, Glenalmond

Alexander stared down at his wife who was crouched between a bush of her namesake and other plants he'd never been able to name. They had never mattered unlike his Marigold. He silently cursed himself for being a fool, he'd been so afraid of her not loving him or of him being unable to be loved that he had been so stunned when she had confessed her love for him he hadn't known what to say nor how to confess his feelings to her.

"Little flower."

Mary started and whirled around to find her husband standing behind her. Again, she had not heard him walk up behind her. She was really going to have to ask him how he was so silent on his feet.

"My lord."

Mary was grateful that her tone came out as level, even with all the butterflies and emotions churning her stomach. Mary was surprised to see him flinch at her tone. She knew he did not like it, which was why she had said it, but she had not anticipated his flinch. Mary felt confusion well up within her.

"You left me."

Standing only a few feet apart it was easy for Mary to hear his hushed words.

"I did." Keeping her voice as low as his, Mary waited for his reply.

"Are you coming back?"

Looking at him now she could see the dark stains under his eyes, the travel weary tilt of his body, Mary wondered how he had journeyed here, for she had taken their only working carriage, the others were either unsuitable for such a distance or being repaired.

Mary said nothing. She wasn't even sure if she could. She was confused as to why he was here, at her sister's home. He didn't love her, he had told her he couldn't, and he had no reason to come for her.

Birds and other animals scuttled and chirped in the bushes and woods that surrounded the colourful garden. Neither of them moved, neither dared breathe after his whispered words that hadn't meant to be uttered but had slipped out regardless.

Mary was the first to speak, tentative though the words were.

"I could not have stayed, Alexander. It would have been too painful. You do not love me and I will be okay with that, eventually. I just need you to give me some time to come to terms with it. I am sorry for putting you out like this. Please just give me a couple of weeks here at my sister's and I will come back and be your duchess."

Staring at him as intently, Mary could see the confusion blossom on his face and felt a little better knowing she wasn't the only one who was confused as to what was happening.

Ignoring his wife's silly notion of wanting some time away to come to terms with his rejection. It was if she did not know him at all. Did she really believe that he would let the woman he loved stay in a different country from his for weeks while she came to terms with his 'rejection'? It was time Alexander told his wife the truth, starting with confessing his love for her. However, before he could open his mouth, his little flower decided to try his temper.

Unaware of her husband's conflicted thoughts, Mary snorted and began her tirade, fuelled only by her stubborn pride that would not let him see her break down.

"Alexander, it's okay. I know you only married me to save my reputation. I don't know why I thought you would love me, I know I'm nothing special. It's okay. I will get over the fact that you don't love me back but, Alexander, if you take a mistress please be discreet for I could not bear th—"

She was cut off by Alexander gripping her arms, his nose inches from hers. Mary had been so busy trying to remain in control of her emotions that she hadn't noticed when Alexander's emotions had got the best of him. Eyes flashing with the anger he was feeling, he shook his wife, who obviously didn't have an ounce of sense in her pretty little head.

Calming himself slightly, Alexander looked into his wife's eyes as he said, "Listen to what I am about to tell you, little flower, because I will not repeat myself."

Barely breathing, Mary looked into her husband's intense eyes and held her breath, waiting for what he would say next.

"I love you. I've loved you since we were children and you would follow me and Charles around, wanting to play with us. I have loved you since you got your silly little self-stuck in a tree! You are my life, I married you because I love you and I wanted you to be mine. And if you ever talk about either of us having a lover I will take you over my knee. You are mine and I am yours."

Frustrated, he released his vexing wife and dragged a hand through his hair. He was going to have to tell her.

"Devil take it Mary! My father hated me, I was the reason his beloved wife was dead. He sent me away the first chance he could and before that I lived with nannies and the servants. If I hadn't been his heir, he'd have disinherited me and said I was not his. I am sure of it. He loved her with all of his being, there was no room left for me."

Once he started, it all came pouring out of him and he couldn't stop talking, not when he noticed Mary crying and not when he felt himself tearing up. He told her how he'd spent many summers alone in his family home, the one she had brought back to life, avoiding his father and wishing he had someone to play with, he told her how moving to his grandparents' house was the best thing to ever happen to him. He told her that moving next door to them as an unloved child was the best thing to ever happen to him.

Tears slipped down both their faces, but neither moved, they didn't know how to close the gap that had been made by insecurity and their own fears.

Mary looked at her husband, the man in front of her telling her that no one had ever told him they loved him before. This caring, generous and amazing man had never been told how amazing he was.

"I love you Alexa—"

Again Mary's sentence was cut short, however this time, her husband wasn't gripping her in desperation and anger. No, he was kissing her and endeavouring to show her just how much he loved her in that one kiss.

"Oh, little flower, my sweet, sweet Marigold." Murmuring her name over and over, Alexander kept kissing his wife, her face, her lips, her neck. At every part of her that wasn't covered, he reigned in kisses, all the while repeating over and over how much he loved her. Mary laughed into his mouth and smacked her husband on the arm at the use of her name, although she could not bring herself to end their kiss. She had never before felt so blissfully happy. He loved her, and she loved him. Always had. Always would.

# Epilogue

## 14 April 1814, Henwood

She was pregnant! Mary had suspected so when her monthly course had not come the previous month. But she did not believe it until the doctor had confirmed her suspicions. She was pregnant. After Alexander had found her in Scotland they had spent a few weeks with her sister, working through their newly expressed feeling for one another and playing with Mary's new, and handsome, nephew.

Alexander had struggled at first to tell her he loved her but Mary did not mind for she knew he loved her. He showed her in the way he would pull her into his arms as they passed in the hall, how he would go visiting tenants for the day and, when she did not accompany him, he would bring her flowers he had picked on his way home. Mary suspected that she had always known he loved her but insecurities and the circumstances of their marriage blinded her. Since Alexander had confided in her about his father, Mary had felt lighter. She now understood her husband completely. They had their moments where they argued, but their arguments were usually just a way to blow off some steam and keep their minds sharp. Mary secretly loved their arguments as Alexander would always take her into his arms and kiss her soundly when they were finished arguing.

"Little flower." Even after over a year of marriage, Mary would never get used to how light on his feet her husband was. One minute he was outside the door speaking with the doctor and the next he was beside her and whispering in her ear.

"One day, Alexander, I am going to sneak up on you!"

"You can sneak up on me anytime you wish, Marigold."

Too excited about telling her husband about their babe, Mary decided to let his use of her full name go.

"What did the doctor say? Does he know why you have been so tired and ill?"

He looked so worried and scared that Mary felt her heart go out to him.

"Yes, yes he does. Although he thinks it will be another seven months before I am completely well again."

"Seven months! That is unacceptable. You cannot do anything, you have not been able to visit the tenants with me in weeks and I know you love that."

He strode to the door, intent on finding that so-called doctor and telling him exactly how unimpressed he was with his service. Mary's laughter stopped him, partly because she had been so tired that he had not heard her laugh in days and he missed it.

"Alexander, there is nothing the doctor can do."

Looking at his wife, who had only just managed to choke out her reply through her laughter, Alexander was very confused.

"Can you tell me what is so funny please, wife?"

His frosty tone did nothing to dull her laughter, she was just so delighted. No, it was the concern she heard in his voice that stopped her.

"Come." Holding out her arms for Alexander, Mary waited for him to take her hands and sit beside her on the bed before she took a deep breath to calm her sudden nerves.

"Alexander, I am pregnant." To say he was stunned by his wife's announcement may have been an understatement. However, that lasted for seconds before he had his wife in his arms and was kissing every inch of her face, unable to contain his excitement.

They laid upon their bed for the rest of the day, kissing, cuddling and discussing the bundle of joy that was currently growing inside Mary's stomach. Mary was just about to fall asleep when Alexander made her smile.

"You realise, little flower, that you may have to share your name for if we have a girl, I may just have two little flowers.

Although our little girl will not be getting herself stuck up a tree."

"Of course not, my dear husband, her mother will be up there with her."

Giving him a cheeky grin Mary snuggled into her husband's hold and decided she was the luckiest woman alive.